D0967025

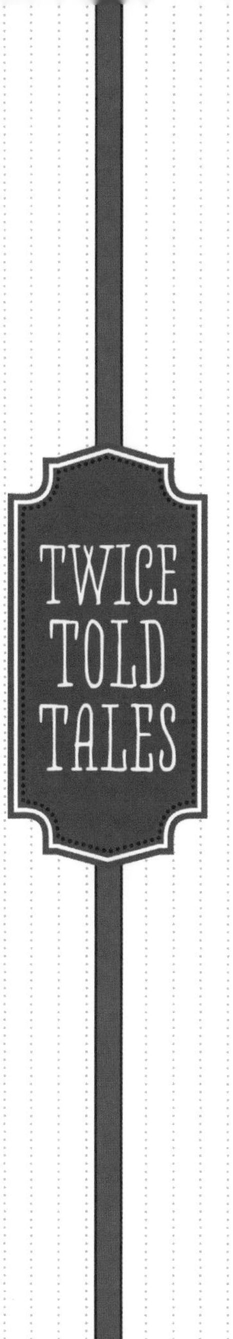
TWICE
TOLD
TALES

Twicetold Tales is published by Stone Arch Books
A Capstone Imprint
1710 Roe Crest Drive
North Mankato, Minnesota 56003
www.capstonepub.com

© 2015 Stone Arch Books

All rights reserved. No part of this publication may be reproduced in whole or in part, or stored in a retrieval system, or transmitted in any form or by any means, electronic, mechanical, photocopying, recording, or otherwise, without written permission of the publisher.

Library of Congress Cataloging-in-Publication Data
Snowe, Olivia, author.
Beauty and the basement / by Olivia Snowe; illustrated by Michelle Lamoreaux.
pages cm. -- (Twicetold tales)
Summary: In this modern version of Beauty and the Beast, unhappy fifteen-year-old Carlo has been living in the basement of his family's mansion ever since his father died—until beautiful fifteen-year-old Belle shows up to pay for the rose her father picked in the garden.
ISBN 978-1-4342-9145-5 (library binding) -- ISBN 978-1-4342-9830-0 (paper-over-board) -- ISBN 978-1-4342-9149-3 (pbk.) -- ISBN 978-1-4965-0082-3 (ebook)
1. Beauty and the beast (Tale)--Juvenile fiction. 2. Fairy tales. 3. Bereavement in adolescence--Juvenile fiction. 4. Parent and child--Juvenile fiction. [1. Fairy tales. 2. Blessing and cursing--Fiction.] I. Lamoreaux, Michelle, illustrator. II. Title.
PZ8.S41763Be 2014
[Fic]--dc23
2013045578

Designer: Kay Fraser
Vector Images: Shutterstock

Printed in China.
032014 8116WAIF14

Beauty and the Basement

by Olivia Snowe

illustrated by Michelle Lamoreaux

STONE ARCH BOOKS™

You know the story.
You've heard it before.
Everyone has.
Now, read it again.
A new twist. A new gasp.
The story is told again.

TWICETOLD.

CARLO

I'm in the basement again. It's dark down here, and it smells like mildew and dryer sheets. Light flickers at me from the huge flat screen mounted on the far wall. It faces my couch. Well, I call it a couch. It might as well be a bed. I sleep down here. I eat down here. I play video games down here. I—

"Carlo!" It's my mother. I don't bother responding. "You've been down there all summer!" she says. "Are you coming upstairs ever again?"

"Not if I can help it," I mutter to myself. Maybe she'll just assume I'm sleeping with the television on. Her high heels clomp down the bare wood stairs. I quickly roll to my side and close my eyes to fake sleep.

"I know you're awake," she says. "I heard the channels changing."

"Fine," I say. "What do you want?"

"I'm going out now," she says. I open one eye first, then the other. She's in a fancy black suit, with her dark hair blown out in ridiculous waves. She's wearing tons of makeup, too.

"Have fun," I say.

She puts a hand on her hip and sighs at me. "What will you do for dinner?" she asks. I lift the remote and switch from some action movie with a guy in a suit to an action movie with a guy in a tank top. I shrug.

"I'll ask Santino to make something for you," she says. Santino's our chef. He lives somewhere in the south wing, I think.

"I can make something myself," I say. It's true. I can. I am an expert at preparing all types of cereal.

"Then I'll give Santino the night off," she replies.

"Whatever," I say, and I push the volume button up with my thumb. "Bye!"

The next thing I hear is the front door slamming.

"Great," I say to myself after the house is quiet. "Now I'm hungry." I swear I wouldn't have even thought of food if Mom hadn't mentioned supper.

I push myself up off the couch and manage to get upstairs. The orangey light in the kitchen means it's after seven. It also means it's late August. It also means school starts next week. I'm not ready for that.

I pour myself a bowl of something colorful and sweet with a little plastic toy inside of the box. Then I lean on the kitchen counter to eat.

"Ah!" says Santino as he steps into the kitchen. "I would have made you something."

"It's all right," I say.

"This sugary garbage," he says, "is *not* all right. I could have made that pasta from last week you liked so much."

My eyebrows shoot up. I love his food. I just don't like the idea of being waited on, like Mom and I are some kind of royalty. We're not. We're two fools living in a ridiculous mansion that neither of us paid for. We're just lucky because Dad was very, very rich.

Was.

Santino obviously sees my interest in his pasta, because he gives me a big grin. Even though he's already hung up his apron, he grabs a pot from under the counter.

"Penne with vodka sauce," he says. "Fresh peas. A little cream."

"You don't have to do this, Santino," I say,

but I'm already ditching my cereal. "You're off the clock."

"Please, please," he says. "I'm happy to. What am I going to do tonight anyway? Fall asleep in front of the TV? What fun is that?"

Well, it's not that *bad,* I think.

"You know I'm happy to make a good supper for you and Mrs. Mostro," he says, "any time."

"Thanks, Santino," I say.

"Now get out of here," he says, turning his back to me and strapping the apron on again. I'm about to head right back downstairs when the doorbell rings. It makes me jump.

I turn and watch Santino at the counter, chopping pancetta. "Well?" I say. He's not the butler; he's the chef. Still, when he's around, he usually answers the door. And with our housekeeper Catalina off till after Labor Day, I really expect him to step up. But no.

"Ah-ah!" Santino says, not even bothering to turn from the cutting board to look at me. "I'm off the clock."

I laugh, but he's not kidding. "You expect *me* to open the door?" I say. Santino pretends he can't hear, continuing to chop and whistle to himself. So I shove through the swinging kitchen door into the big entryway. Lightning cracks outside—I didn't even know it had started raining.

When I open the door, a man rushes right past me, his coat pulled up over his head.

"Whoa!" I say, flinching at the spray as he shakes off.

"I'm terribly sorry to bother you at this hour," he shouts over the thunder. "Car trouble."

Santino comes through the swinging door, wiping his hands on a dish towel.

"Sir," the stranger says, moving to shake Santino's hand. "I'm so sorry for bursting in. If

I could just use your phone, I'm happy to wait outside."

He thinks Santino is my dad. It reminds me of what I've tried to forget. My dad is dead.

"I'll show you the way to the phone," I say, stepping between them. "Mr. . . . ?"

"Forgive me. I'm Jack Beaumont," he says. He stands up straight for the first time since he burst in. He has a graying blond mustache. He pulls off his hat to reveal a head of thinning hair, the same shade as his mustache.

"I'm Carlo," I say. "This is my house. And this"—I thumb at Santino—"is our chef." I pause, thinking for a minute.

"Don't you have a cell phone?" I ask.

"Ah," he says, looking away from me. "The battery died. Darn thing." He forces a smile and a shrug. For some reason, I think he's lying.

"Follow me," I say. I lead Mr. Beaumont through the kitchen, through the back door to the courtyard, and out to my mother's greenhouse. We have other phones, but the greenhouse is the only room enclosed in windows. That means I can keep an eye on him from the kitchen.

"Right here," I say, gesturing to Mom's wicker patio set, with a phone on the side table. "I'll let you have some privacy."

He thanks me and sits down. I pull up my hood and dart across the courtyard to the kitchen. I sit on the stool by the window to watch Mr. Beaumont. He has the phone cradled under his ear, and he's wandering through Mom's prize-winning indoor garden. Now and then he stops to read a label or take a leaf between his thumb and forefinger, like he's testing the quality of a piece of fabric.

"I shouldn't have let him in," I say to Santino.

He sighs. "Maybe," he says. "But this is some storm."

BELLE

~2~

I *can't imagine what's keeping Dad*, I think as I sit in my bedroom. Well, sort of my bedroom. It was Dad's office until my room upstairs sprung a leak in the ceiling. Now I sleep in Dad's office.

Not that he needs it. His business went belly-up two years ago when one of his planes crashed in the middle of the Pacific Ocean. It was carrying most of the company's merchandise. When it was lost, Dad was responsible. He went bankrupt. Since then, we've lived modestly. This once-magnificent brownstone on one of the most beautiful blocks in the city is crumbling.

But tonight I feel hopeful. Dad had an important meeting out by the ocean, near the big homes and the cute villages with fudge shops.

The phone rings and I dive to grab it. "Dad?"

"Hello, Belle," he says. I can hear the disappointment in his voice.

"What happened?" I say. I hate the sound of my own voice, full of disapproval. I imagine that I sound like a scolding mother. But my mom died when I was young. I don't even remember the sound of her voice.

"Just a little mishap with the car," he says. "Belle, the ocean here under the moonlight is positively breathtaking."

"Where are you?" I ask.

"Just waiting for the tow truck," Dad says. He takes a loud, long breath through his nose, like he's smelling something.

"Where are you waiting?" I ask.

"The most amazing house," Dad says. "It's the sort of house you'd love, on a hill overlooking the ocean. I can hear the waves crashing from here."

"Whose house is it?" I ask.

"I didn't get the last name," Dad says. He seems distracted. He sniffs again and sighs.

"Dad," I say. "What do you keep sniffing?"

"Flowers," he says. "I'm in a greenhouse."

At the very word, I feel like I'm there too, surrounded by winding paths through the ornate glass wing of the estate, each path greener and more floral than the last. There are even butterflies, and it's warm and smells sweet inside. I'm jealous, and Dad knows it.

"I'm sorry, sweetheart," he says. "I wish

you could see this place. The roses"—he actually gasps—"the flowers are so big and fragrant. It's intoxicating."

"Red ones?" I ask.

"Red ones," he says. Then he adds in a whisper. "Perhaps . . . perhaps you *can* see one."

"Dad," I say. I know what he's thinking. "Don't."

"Oh, you worry too much," he says. "They won't miss one little bud."

But I know my dad, and he won't pick some little bud. He'll pick the biggest, most beautiful flower in the greenhouse. "Dad, please don't," I say. "What if you get caught?"

Dad laughs. "By who?" he says. "The cook or the teenager? Trust me, Belle. It'll be fine."

CARLO

~3~

"I'll kill him," I growl, marching toward the kitchen door to the courtyard.

"Carlo," Santino says, grabbing my elbow. "Try to stay calm. I'll speak to him."

I pull my arm away and throw open the door, stomping outside. It's still storming, and rain blows into the kitchen.

White light cracks across the sky. Thunder booms—the perfect soundtrack for my rage.

Then lightning cracks again, this time right overhead, as I enter the greenhouse.

"How dare you!" I roar.

Mr. Beaumont jumps at the sound, dropping the phone and the rose he's stolen from my mother's prize-winning crop. His jaw drops too, and he throws up his hands.

I grab him by the lapel of his jacket and lift him six inches off the ground, so we're eye to eye. "P-p-please," he stammers, his voice high and thin, like a frightened child's. "I meant no harm."

I give him a shake. "Those are my mother's prize-winning roses," I snarl. "They're worth a fortune—in money and time and pride."

"I didn't know," he says. "I thought—I thought my daughter might like one."

I give him another shake. "You should have asked," I say. Then I toss him to the rubber mat on the ground.

He looks up at me, covering his face with his arms. "Please," he says. "I just took it for my daughter. I'm very sorry. She just loves flowers so much and I can't afford to . . ."

He's petrified. Terrified. Of *me*.

I haven't always been an angry, violent guy. I don't know what comes over me sometimes. I become a monster. I take a few deep breaths to clear my head.

"I'm calling the police," I say, and I move to pick up the phone from the ground. I can hear a girl's voice on the other end of the line. Mr. Beaumont grabs my wrist.

"Please," he says. "Don't call the police. I couldn't live with the shame. And my poor daughter . . ."

I grab the phone, but instead of hanging up and calling the police, I put it to my ear. There's someone shouting. "Stop," I say into the phone. The line goes silent, aside from some nervous breathing. "How old are you?"

"Um," says the girl. I assume it's Mr. Beaumont's daughter. "Fifteen."

I hang up. "You can go," I say. "I won't call the police. Heck, you can keep that flower."

Mr. Beaumont slowly stands up. "Thank you," he says. "You've been so generous, I—"

"I wasn't done," I say. I grab him under the arm and lead him back into the house. "Our housekeeper has another week of vacation left," I say as we reach the front door. "And the house is in a dreadful state."

Mr. Beaumont's head swivels as he looks around. "It looks okay to me," he says.

I ignore him. "Your daughter will make up for it," I say. "Send her here tomorrow. She will clean the house for the rest of the week, and the rose will be paid for."

"A week of labor for a single flower?" he says, shocked.

"Would you rather I call the police?" I say.

He stands up straighter. "No," he says.

Now *I* am shocked. Will Mr. Beaumont agree to this absurd plan? I only meant to humiliate him.

"If that is what it will take to renew my family's honor, then so be it," he says proudly.

"Fine," I say, and I open the front door for him. Orange and yellow lights flash across the front of the house.

"A tow truck has arrived for me," Mr. Beaumont says. "Thank you for your hospitality." He bows to me as he departs. "My daughter will be at your door first thing tomorrow morning."

"See that she is," I say, closing the door behind him. I watch from the front window as he climbs into the tow truck's cab.

I don't believe for a moment that the old loser's daughter will actually show up. But it was fun to make him squirm a little.

BELLE

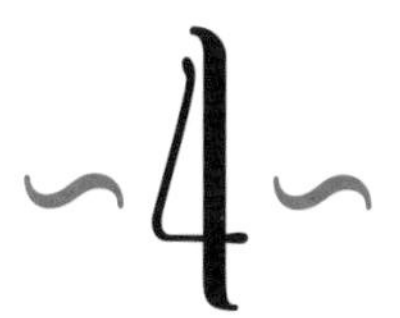

Dad still isn't home, and I'm tired of waiting. Shouldn't *he* be the one worrying and waiting up for me?

I pull my phone from my pocket. It doesn't work as a phone though. Some expenses just had to be cut, and that included cell phones. But the phone's clock works, and sometimes I use the Wi-Fi from the café across the street.

It's ten o'clock when I hear keys jingle outside the front door. I pull it open before Dad can get it unlocked. "Finally!" I snap. He jumps. "Do you know how worried I've been?"

Instead of apologizing and offering an explanation for disappearing from our phone call, Dad holds out a single long-stemmed rose.

"For my Belle," he says, smiling.

I wish I could explain what comes over me when Dad gives me a rose. All the anger that's been bubbling up inside me, pacing in the front hall for the last hour and a half, fizzles away. I take the rose and put it to my lips so I can feel the softness of its petals and let its perfect fragrance fill my nose.

"It's beautiful," I say.

"My dear, what an evening I've had," Dad says. There's laughter in his voice.

"I don't understand why you're in such a good mood," I say. "Your meeting went terribly. You wrecked the car. And who knows what happened in that house!"

In an instant, Dad is bent over laughing, slapping his legs. His face is bright red.

"Tell me what's so funny!" I demand.

So he does. He tells me about the crash—how he'd had his eyes on the ocean under the sunset and didn't see the curve in the road. He tells me about the mansion on the hill above the beach. He tells me about the awful young man—dark hair, dark eyes, dark mood.

"He was a beast," Dad says as I follow him into the living room. He sits in his old recliner. "Ill-tempered. Violent. Just extremely irritable."

"Sounds like a monster," I say, sitting on the arm of the chair.

Dad puts an arm around me. "I haven't told you the best part. He caught me helping myself to that one rose—not even that special, really. I've seen hundreds like it."

I nod, but it's not true. The rose Dad brought home tonight is extraordinary. I've never seen a rose so red, with petals so fine.

"He fell into a mad rage!" Dad says. "I thought he might tear me to pieces with his bare hands!"

I gasp, on cue. "But then he seemed to calm down," Dad goes on, "and he made the most amusing suggestion. He'd let me go unharmed, and he'd even let me bring that ordinary rose home to you, on one condition. That *you*," he says, taking my chin in his hand, "go and work for him as a *maid!*"

He stares up at me, his mouth open in an amused grin, as if expecting me to laugh right along with him. Instead, I slide off the arm of the chair and put my hands on my hips. "Are you kidding?" I say. "The nerve . . ."

"I know!" Dad says. He gets up and walks to the bookshelf at the far wall. That's where he keeps his fancy scotch—the only trace of his wealth that remains. "Astounding," he says as he pours his drink. "Well, it was that or—get this—he'd call the cops. All for a lousy rose!"

"He *didn't!*" I say, leaning forward. "He called the police?"

Dad cocks his left eyebrow in that funny way he has. It must've been charming when he was a young man.

"Of course not," he says. "I told him you'd be happy to come clean, and then I hopped into the tow truck." He sips his drink. I stare at him. "What?" he says.

"You told him I'd . . ." I say, not able to believe it.

"Oh, Belle," he says, "I certainly never meant for you to actually go there to clean." He takes another sip. "The idea," he says. "My Belle Beaumont should clean that showy mansion for a loud, pushy son of social climbers? I think not."

"Then you lied," I say, my voice quiet.

"Hmm?" he says, looking at me through the bottom of his tumbler.

"You lied," I repeat.

"I suppose I did," Dad says, shrugging. "What would you have me do now? Call the police? Turn myself in for stealing a rose?"

"That won't be necessary," I say. "I intend to keep the promise you made."

"What?" Dad says. "You can't be serious."

"I'd better get to bed so I can catch the early train to the beach," I say, heading upstairs.

He laughs. "But dear, you don't know the address."

* * *

In the morning, I'm up with the sun. I hear Dad's loud snores as I creep past his room. I hurry down the steps, find his coat, and dig in the pockets. It's as I guessed: the tow truck receipt is there, folded and wrinkled but very much legible. Now I have the address. By the time Dad wakes up, I'll be at the mansion on the hill above the ocean.

CARLO

5

I'm dreaming. It's thundering in the dream, and there are voices—Mom and Dad. Mom is shouting. "Dad is back!" I scream at her. Back from the dead, I mean. "Don't shout at him!"

Then there's another voice—a voice I don't know. A girl's voice.

It wakes me, and I sit up on the couch in the dark basement to find my blanket and pillows on the floor—and shouting coming down through the ceiling. I can hear Santino and Mom.

And then there's the girl's voice—quiet, almost timid. I can't make out what she's saying. Especially with Santino and Mom yelling over her.

"It's too early!" Mom shouts.

Mom usually speaks in a shout. Sometimes an excited shout, sometimes an angry shout, sometimes a shout of sorrow, but almost always a shout. "My head is pounding. My feet are throbbing. Explain yourself."

The girl replies, but it's a murmur. Santino's gentle, deep voice interjects now and then: "It's true," he says. "Ah," he adds. "Of course, of course," he agrees.

"I don't know anyone named Beaumont," Mom says. I sit up a little straighter.

Beaumont. It begins to come back to me—what happened last night.

"Carlo," Santino says. His voice is comforting. "He knows what this is about."

I sure do, I think as I pull on yesterday's jeans. Barefoot and wrinkled from sleep, I make my way upstairs to the entryway, pushing my way through the swinging door and running a hand through my greasy, floppy mess of hair.

"*There* you are," says Mom when she spots me, and the swinging door hits me in the back when it closes.

Mom's in her dark green terrycloth robe and slippers. She's got one hand on her hip and another on her head. She had a late night, apparently. Santino is in his chef's whites, a towel on his shoulder and an omelet pan in his hand.

And between them, with hair the color of maple leaves in October and eyes as gray as the sky over the ocean during a storm, is the most beautiful girl I've ever seen.

BELLE

I've been standing in the entryway of this house for the last three minutes being yelled at by a woman who'd fit right in on a reality show about rich housewives. And there's a chef who pops in once in a while with a know-it-all remark.

Now this boy is staring at me from the doorway. He's my age, but he looks like he hasn't seen the sun in years. His hair is wild and greasy. His clothes are stained and wrinkled.

The kitchen door swings closed behind him and knocks him in the back. I giggle. I can't help it.

"*There* you are," the woman says to him. He's her son, I assume. "Do you know what this girl wants?"

"I'll handle it," the boy says. His voice is quiet and gruff.

"Good," the woman says, walking away. "I'm going back to bed."

"Ah, well," says the chef. "Carlo, this is—"

"Just go make me breakfast, Santino," says the boy—Carlo, apparently.

"Of course," Santino says. He smiles at me and slips past Carlo into the kitchen.

"I didn't think you'd actually show up," Carlo says, crossing his arms.

"My dad didn't want me to come," I say. I'm trying to appear confident and calm, but I didn't think this through. Am I really going to spend the last few days of my summer vacation cleaning the huge home of a very rude family?

"But I believe in keeping promises," I continue. "Even to a beast like you."

"A beast?" he says.

"You'd have to be a monster," I say, "to force a girl to be a servant because of a single silly rose."

He narrows his eyes and stares at me a moment too long. "What's your name?"

"Belle," I say.

He grunts and turns his back on me. "Cleaning stuff is in this closet," he says, banging his fist on the closet door. "You can start in the dining room. It's always dusty."

He puts a hand on the kitchen door to leave and then stops, looking at me over his shoulder. "Stay out of the greenhouse," he says. He pushes the door open and calls back, "And the basement!"

CARLO

7

"This is insane," I mumble. I'm pacing in the basement, and upstairs is a girl. A girl my age. A beautiful girl my age.

"Can that really be her name?" I say to myself, falling backward onto the couch. I pick up the remote and click on the TV. "Belle—like a fairy-tale princess? It's too much."

I can't believe how quickly I'm crushing on this girl. There was this feeling I had in my chest when I saw her face—kind of like someone had taken my heart and squeezed it. It's all I've felt besides sadness or anger for the last five months.

"I have to see her again," I whisper. Rather than run up from the basement to find her in the dining room, I simply switch inputs on the TV to access the house's closed-circuit security system.

Cameras. They're all over the house. We never use them, really. Now and then I'll check them to make sure the kitchen is empty before I sneak up there for a midnight snack. But otherwise, they're strictly for security. If someone were to break in, we'd have full-color photos of the criminal.

I click to the dining room camera, and there she is. She has a rag in one hand and a bottle of polish in the other. She sprays the table and wipes it down.

Eventually she leaves the dining room. I have to click through the cameras to find her.

When I do, she's in the living room, pushing the vacuum across the carpeted floor.

I've been wasting my time staring at the surveillance channels for far too long when I realize I'm hungry again. It must be almost lunchtime. I'm thinking of sticking my head into the kitchen when Belle disappears from the living room.

I click through all the channels—kitchen, dining room, upstairs, greenhouse, Mom's workout room, rear grounds—and find no sign of her.

I'm hungry anyway. I might as well go up and ask Santino to make lunch. Maybe I'll catch a glimpse of Belle while I'm up there. I click the TV off and head upstairs.

I'm almost to the top of the basement steps when the door flies open, sending me sprawling back down the wooden stairs, and onto the carpeted basement floor.

BELLE

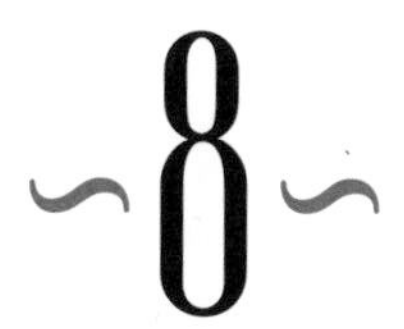

"Oh!" I say. I reach for him—much too late. Then my hands go to my mouth as he tumbles down the steps and to the basement floor. "I'm so sorry!"

"What are you doing?!" he snarls up at me. "I told you to stay out of the basement!"

"I'm really sorry," I say. He's not hurt—just embarrassed. He should be, too. Not because he fell, but because the basement is a dank and disgusting place, smelling of old laundry and tomato sauce. And I get the feeling he spends all his time down here.

"Did you finish cleaning the living room?" he snaps as he gets to his feet.

"Living room?" I say, because he asked me to clean the dining room, not the living room. I did some cleaning in the living room, too, but how would he know that?

"I mean the dining room," he says, looking away from me. "Did you or not?"

"Yes," I say, "but I came to tell you that I'm leaving now."

"Already?" he says. I can't tell if he's angry that I haven't done more work or just disappointed that I'm leaving.

"Yes," I say. "I have a job at the hospital in the afternoons. The trip back to the city is very long on buses and trains and all that."

"Oh," he says. "Fine, then." He starts up the

stairs toward me and puts a hand on the door, as if to slam it in my face.

"I'll be back tomorrow morning," I say. And it's true. I'll keep my dad's promise, even if it's insane. Dad needs to know what it means to be honest in business, and I need to show him.

"You better," Carlo growls. "And the day after that, too, and after that—till our housekeeper Catalina is back."

"I will," I say, and I quickly step back as Carlo slams the basement door, barely missing my toes.

"What nerve," I mutter to myself as I turn away from the basement door, and there's Santino, watching me. Watching us. He looks away quickly.

"It's fine, Santino," I say. "You have a right to keep your ears and eyes unplugged while you're in your own kitchen."

I lean on the marble island and stare at the Mediterranean tile floor, which I'll probably

have to clean in the morning. I hope Santino isn't a messy cook.

"He's been through a lot lately," Santino whispers. "Try not to hold it against him."

"He makes it very difficult," I say, sighing.

Santino suddenly brightens. "Here," he says, and he grabs a paper-wrapped parcel, holding it out to me. "Lunch."

"Oh, I shouldn't," I say. "I really have to get going. The bus will be by in a few minutes."

"I made it to-go," Santino says.

Whatever he's been cooking in here all morning smells amazing. If this is even a tiny sampling of that, it'll be the best lunch I've had in ages. "Thank you," I say. "It's very nice of you." He waves me off, like I shouldn't mention it.

"I really should go now," I say, heading out of the kitchen. "I'll see you tomorrow."

"Tomorrow!" he calls after me.

CARLO

I cannot believe that chef of ours. He's just given her lunch!

I hear her footsteps hurrying through the house. I hear the front door close when she leaves.

An instant later, the basement door creaks, and a sliver of light from the kitchen pokes into my sanctuary.

"What do you want?" I snap. I don't know if it's Mom or Santino, but it makes no difference.

"Hello, *luce del sole*," Santino says. It means "sunshine" in Italian. He's hilarious. He's carrying a tray, which means it's lunchtime.

"I don't want it," I say, turning the TV on.

"Who says this is for you?" Santino cracks. "Maybe I'm planning to eat my lunch down here in front of the TV. Ever think of that?"

See? He's hilarious.

He puts the tray down on the small table next to the couch. "Look. Eat something. You seem extra grumpy today."

I turn up the volume.

"Is it because of the girl?" Santino shouts over the blaring TV. So I turn it up even louder. He grabs the remote from me and turns it off.

"She's very nice," Santino says. "And very pretty."

"Go back upstairs," I say.

Santino sighs. "You know," he says, "she could be the one."

"The one?" I repeat because I don't know what he's talking about.

"The one to break the curse," Santino says. "The curse of the boy who has locked himself away in the basement of misery and despair for these last five months."

"Go upstairs," I repeat.

"I'm just saying . . ."

So now I roar at him: "Go upstairs!"

He finally retreats, his palms turned up and a fake apologetic grin on his face.

BELLE

10

When I get home after eight o'clock, my back and feet are sore, and my hands are callused and cramped. I open the front door and see Dad pacing across the living room floor. He looks worried.

"Finally!" he shouts, his face turning red.

So maybe he wasn't worried . . . just mad.

"Do you know the state I've been in all day?" he shouts.

I slide past him and hobble over to the beat-up couch in the living room, falling onto it with a sigh.

"I was worried sick," he says.

I manage to lift my eyes to glare at him. "Why?" I say.

"Who knew what might have happened to you!" he says.

"You knew where I was," I reply with my last ounce of strength.

"I sure did," he says. "Which is the other thing. You disobeyed me."

"Mmhmm," I mumble. "And you lied."

"To a stranger!" he says. "To save my reputation."

"Ha!" I say, lifting my head to face him. "I saved your reputation by keeping your stupid promise!"

Dad snorts and sits heavily in his recliner, and I drop my head back again. I can feel him

glaring at me from all the way across the living room.

"Well, you won't go back again," Dad says. "You've made your point. Now stop this foolishness. A girl your age, working as a maid *and* a hospital orderly. It's inappropriate."

"So is lying," I say, "and making promises you have no intention to keep."

"Enough!" he snaps. "No more, is that clear?"

"It's clear," I say, "but now *I've* made a promise—to go back until their housekeeper returns—and I intend to keep it."

"You're crazy," Dad says.

I take a deep breath and push myself up into a seated position. "The boy who lives there," I say. "Carlo. He's something, isn't he?"

"I had the pleasure," Dad says sarcastically.

"He really is awful, huh?" I say, remembering the tone in the boy's voice and the anger on his face. But I also remember what Santino said, and I remember Carlo's tone when I told him I had to leave and he said, "Already?"

"He probably just needs a friend," I say. I don't even mean to say it aloud. I'm not even sure I believe it. Dad sure doesn't. He laughs—a short, dismissive laugh.

"Well, it's true," I say. "I mean, locked away in that house, in the dark basement, with only his crazy mother and their chef for company. Of course he's miserable."

"Maybe he does need a friend," Dad says. "But it sure doesn't need to be you."

"I think I can get through to him," I say.

Dad groans. "I had a very long day," he says. "I'm going to bed." He kisses my forehead. "I suppose you'll be gone before I'm awake?"

"Unless you're up before five," I say, blowing him a kiss.

CARLO

~11~

I'm on the balcony this morning, looking down at the driveway. When the doorbell rings, I step back against the wall. I hear Santino hurry for the door. "Just a second," he calls. Then he pulls open the door. "Ciao, Bella!" he says.

"Good morning, Santino," Belle says as she steps inside.

There's that feeling in my chest again, only this time, the hand that takes my heart and squeezes it holds on just a little longer, and my breath is gone for just a little longer. When I can breathe again, I gasp and cough.

Santino and Belle both look up and find me on the balcony, looking down at them.

"Start in the library today," I roar down. "It'll probably take all morning. It's covered in dust."

"Some people," Belle says, holding my gaze with her stony-gray eyes, "open with things like 'hello,' or 'good morning.'"

I throw my hands onto the railing and shout down at her, "Library!" Then I turn my back on them and open my bedroom door.

I've hardly been in here all summer. In fact, as I sit on the edge of the bed and stare at the desk across the room, I realize I haven't been in here at all in five months.

My action figures are still there on my desk, lined up in a neat row. There are books there, too—stories of monsters, knights, dragons, elves, trolls, and kings. I used to love reading books.

Last winter, when Dad was already sick—though we didn't know it yet—he and I spent the cold months passing our favorite books back and forth. Now I can hardly look at them.

There's a photo in a plain red frame on the desk. I'd forgotten about that photo. It's Mom, smiling and happy, and me, around nine or ten years old. And with his arm around me, there's Dad. He looks exhausted and happy. It was the last day of our Caribbean vacation on Dad's weekender yacht. He was both captain and crew.

I actually smile for an instant, remembering the vacation and remembering Dad. But the tiny spotlight of happiness isn't strong enough to push out the anger and the sadness. I lift the picture over my head and slam it against the desktop. The glass shatters into a hundred pieces.

BELLE

~12~

Smash! I jump at the sound coming from upstairs. Santino flinches a little, but he hardly seems to notice.

"He's been so unhappy," Santino says. He's leading me through the house to the library. As we're walking down a long hallway, decorated with paintings and photographs from all over the world, Santino stops.

"His father passed away," he says quietly.

"Oh, I'm sorry," I say, and I truly am. I

should have guessed something traumatic happened to him.

"Carlo is a sensitive boy," Santino says as he starts walking down the hallway again.

I follow along, all the while thinking, *Carlo? Sensitive?*

"To tell you the truth," Santino says as we reach a pair of closed doors at the end of the hallway, "I was surprised he asked you to clean the library."

Santino pulls a key from his pocket, unlocks the doors, then pushes them open. "Because no one ever comes in here," he says. "It was Mr. Mostro's private sanctuary."

"Wow," I say walking into the room. It's huge, and there are bookshelves everywhere. "I guess Carlo's dad was a big reader."

Santino closes his eyes and nods. "The biggest. Carlo, too." My eyes widen.

"I know it's hard to believe these days,"

Santino continues, laughing, "but he and his father were cut from the same cloth."

"He couldn't possibly have read all these books," I say, turning around the massive room. I love books. I used to buy books all the time, but I haven't since Dad's business failed. Now I go to the library when I can.

"He may have missed a few," Santino says, "but you'd be surprised." He shows me around, explaining, "These are biographies. Here are mysteries—Mr. Mostro's favorites. Here are the fantasy and science fiction stories—Carlo's favorites. World history. Philosophy. Theology. Mythology. It goes on and on."

"It's an amazing collection," I say. "I could spend all morning here, reading instead of cleaning." I add, "I mean, I wouldn't, of course. I'm here to work, like I promised."

Santino chuckles. "Don't be silly," he says. "We all know this arrangement Carlo and your father made is . . . well, it's crazy."

"A little," I say. "But I'll keep my promise."

Santino shrugs as he heads out of the room. "Suit yourself," he says. "I'll be heading back to the kitchen. I wonder what lunch I should pack for you today . . ."

With a smile on my face, I pull the duster from my bucket and start in on the shelves of leather-bound books, reading their spines, some printed in fine gold lettering. There are stories in Italian and English and Latin and Greek and languages I can't identify. There are tales of dragons and spaceships and colonies on Saturn's moons. There are thick volumes of poetry and ancient myths and histories of ancient people who sailed the world's oceans.

It's too much to bear, smelling their paper and glue and bindings, dusting the shelves and the spines, but unable to pull one out to pore over its pages. I think I might burst.

CARLO

~13~

I'm back in the basement, where I can wallow in darkness and think about exactly nothing: not about Dad and our perfect life before he got sick, not about Belle and her perfect face.

I slouch on the comfy basement couch and stare at the huge screen across the room, shooting my way through the hordes of zombies.

It's got to be almost noon when I hear

Santino's knock on the basement door. He doesn't wait for my reply, though. He just throws the door wide open, flooding my basement with light. "Close the door!" I shout.

"Oh, please forgive the interruption," Santino says. He's being sarcastic, of course. "Belle will be leaving in a few minutes. I thought you might like to come upstairs and do something civil for a change, like say goodbye."

"Nah," I say. "Is that all?" I glance at Santino as he rolls his eyes and departs.

The moment the door closes, I switch to the surveillance video and find Belle in the library. But she's not cleaning at all. Instead, she's perched on the edge of one of the red leather chairs near the fireplace, one of Dad's books open on her knees and a stack of books—perhaps ones she's already paged through—on the floor beside her.

I jump up from the couch, roaring as I run upstairs and through the kitchen.

"What's happened?" Santino says, but I ignore him and head for the rear hallway. As I bang open the library doors, she jumps up from the chair.

"What do you think you're doing?!" I growl as I cross the library's huge floor. I stop in front of her, grab the book she is looking through, and slam it down on the pile beside her, sending the tower of books to the floor.

"I'm sorry," she says quietly.

"You're just like your dad," I say. I can feel my face getting hot. "You come into our house, into the spaces that are most precious to my family!" I shout. "You put your filthy hands on the things that matter most to us." She cowers as I scream, but I can't stop yelling. I don't even *want* to stop yelling. "Like you're entitled to everything we have," I say. "But you're not! You couldn't possibly understand what it's like to be us! Because you're nothing! You're worthless!"

And Belle slaps my face. Hard.

BELLE

14

"Ow." Carlo stares at me, holding his hand on his cheek.

"Oh my goodness," I say, putting a hand to my mouth. "I'm sorry."

He turns away from me, so I take his wrist. "Let me see," I say. "I'm so sorry."

"It's fine," Carlo whispers, pulling his arm away from me.

Santino clears his throat in the doorway.

He's been watching us the entire time. "Don't be sorry," he says. "He had it coming."

I shoot Santino a glare, hoping he'll take the hint to leave. He does, but not before he holds up a paper bag and places it on the table by the door. My lunch, to-go.

I put a hand on Carlo's back, and he flinches, but he doesn't pull away. "I'm sorry I hit you," I say. "I have to go now. I'll be back in the morning." I head for the door and grab the paper bag. I look back at Carlo.

"No," he says. "You don't have to come back."

I should be happy. I should simply thank him and never come back.

"No," I say instead. "I'll be back in the morning."

* * *

That night, I dream I'm in a French garden, lost in a maze of rose bushes, stone benches, and fountains. I'm not afraid, though. I'm aware that someone is chasing me. But it's for fun, and I'm laughing. He's laughing, too.

I round a corner in the maze and shriek with laughter as I run smack into him. He laughs too and picks me up in a hug. He has the brightest eyes, full of joy and love—love for me. I know his eyes.

Then the world around us goes black, and I'm alone, still in the garden maze. I'm not laughing anymore. Instead, I'm breathless with fear, afraid to run and afraid to stand still.

I hear my pursuer making his way through the shrubs—he isn't laughing now. He breathes and snarls like a monster, and I cower into the darkest corner I can find, hoping the sun will come out. When I catch a glimpse of the beast as he rounds the corner, I sit up in bed with a start, scared out of the dream.

CARLO

15

I'm awake before Santino this morning. I'm spreading peanut butter on toast when Santino comes into the kitchen wearing his chef's outfit.

"This is a nice surprise," Santino says. He heads toward the coffee pot. "You're up awfully early—or have you not gone to bed yet? I can never tell the difference."

"Ha-ha," I say.

Santino fills the pot with water. "So why

are you up then?" he asks. "Just keeping me company?"

"I'm too angry to sleep," I say.

It's not really true, though—that I'm angry. I mean, it should be true. She actually slapped me across the face.

"Can you believe she hit me?" I say.

"Yes," he says, and at that moment, the doorbell rings.

"I'll get it," I say to Santino, doing my best to make my voice sound strained and angry. But I feel excited.

I run to the entryway, open the door, take a step outside, and say, "Good morning."

Belle is shocked for a moment. "Hello."

"I shouldn't have yelled at you," I say.

"No," she says. She starts to make her way inside. "That wasn't nice."

"But you shouldn't have hit me," I add quickly, making her stop again to look at me.

"Fair enough." She puts out her hand.

"Okay," I say, and we shake hands. She smiles at me, but then I remember that I probably still have peanut butter on my fingers from that toast I was eating, and I pull my hand away quickly.

It's too late. She definitely has some peanut butter on her hand, but she's too polite to say anything about it.

I can feel my face turning red as I wipe my hand on my jeans and head toward the kitchen. "You can clean the rooms upstairs today," I shout to her over my shoulder as I flee. "Start with the bathrooms!"

Then, without stopping to rinse my plate or say anything to a very surprised Santino, I hurry down the basement steps, into my den of solitude.

* * *

I'm watching her on the closed-circuit TV as she cleans the rooms upstairs. She's been in my bedroom—my real bedroom—for a few minutes, poking around.

But I won't yell at her this time. I'm not even sure I care.

And now she's standing in front of my desk, holding the cracked picture frame with the picture of my family . . . from when we were a real family.

And she's crying. She's crying for me.

I don't know why she cares. I've been horrible to her. I've been horrible to her father. I've even been horrible to Santino.

I'm crying now, too. I shake it off and wipe my sleeve across my face. Then I hurry upstairs to the library. The pile of books is still on the floor from yesterday. I grab the one on top—the one Belle had been reading—and I sit down with it at the table.

BELLE

~16~

Maybe it's because I'm finding that I care about him, that I want him to be happier, that I feel like I can help him be happier.

Maybe it's just curiosity.

Whatever it is, it makes me wonder about him. With a glance over my shoulder to make sure no one is watching, I slip into Carlo's bedroom and close the door behind me.

It could be any boy's room—well, any boy

with a collection of action figures, a view of the ocean, a walk-in closet, and a queen-size bed. It's decorated with posters and bookcases and some photographs.

I walk toward the desk beside the big window that looks out over the ocean.

My foot crunches on something, making me flinch. It's a piece of glass—the desk and floor nearby are littered with glass. I've found the only thing in the room in the slightest disarray—a busted picture frame and the photo it held.

There's a woman—Carlo's mother. I hardly recognize her. There's Carlo, an adorable young boy, with a smile bigger than all the outdoors. And there's a man who must be Carlo's dad.

My mother is dead, but I never knew her. It hasn't been easy—growing up without a mother.

Still, I can't imagine pain like that.

I think of Carlo, so deep in darkness, living his life without joy, and my eyes fill with tears. I'm not just crying for him, though. I'm crying for myself and for Dad. I'm crying for Carlo's mother. I'm even crying for Santino.

I let myself sob, just for a moment, and then wipe my eyes with the back of my hand. I know better than to dawdle here when I'm supposed to be cleaning.

* * *

It turns out there are four bathrooms on the second floor. I don't think any of them are in very heavy use, though, aside from the one in Mrs. Mostro's master suite.

I spend most of the morning cleaning it, wondering if Carlo's mom is home someplace in this huge house, or if she's gone out for the morning, or if she simply never came home at all last night.

Around noon, I walk down the main staircase and find Carlo at the bottom, apparently waiting for me. "Um," I say, stopping halfway, "am I in trouble again?" I smile at him so he knows I'm joking.

He's still in the rumpled jeans and hoodie. I wonder if he's washed the peanut butter off his hands. His handshake earlier was sticky, but I know he meant well. He's holding a paper bag and a gift-wrapped package.

"Are you leaving now?" he asks. His voice sounds gruff, but it has the tiniest smidge of friendliness.

"Yes," I say as I finish the trip downstairs. "Bus to catch." I stop in front of him, by the front door. "What's this?" I say, nodding at the packages.

"Lunch," he says, stiffly holding up the paper bag.

"Thank you," I say. "Thank Santino for me, too, please."

He nods, staring at me.

"And that?" I ask, gesturing toward his other hand.

"Oh." He holds the package up in front of him. "It's for you."

I take the package, wrapped in shiny silver paper with a forest-green ribbon.

"Thank you," I say, and I smile at him. I begin to peel away the wrapping, but he takes my hand to stop me.

"Not yet," he says. "Wait until you leave."

"Okay," I say, pleased that his hand is no longer sticky. "Why do I get a present?"

He grunts and shrugs. "Will you be back tomorrow?" he asks.

"Of course," I say.

Carlo reaches past me and opens the door. "Goodbye," he says.

* * *

I reach the bus stop with a few moments to spare and tear off a corner of the silver paper. It's a book—the book I'd been reading yesterday when he found me in the library.

"One of his dad's," I whisper.

CARLO

~17~

I stand in the front hall, watching through the open door as she walks down the driveway to the main road and the bus stop.

Her hair, in the bright afternoon sunlight and blowing in the strong ocean breeze, is shining and waving like a sunset reflected on the water.

I hear the kitchen door swing open before Santino speaks. "That was a very nice thing you did," he says.

"I don't know what you're talking about," I answer.

"Of course you don't," Santino says. "But if you keep this up, that girl might actually stop slapping you."

The kitchen door swings again as Santino retreats to the kitchen. As Belle disappears around the curve at the bottom of the hill, I finally close the front door. I realize my cheeks hurt, just a tiny bit, because I've been smiling since she left.

* * *

"Chicken Marsala!" Santino announces as he comes down the basement steps with dinner.

"Thanks," I say, sitting up on the couch. He puts the tray on the little table in front of me.

"And now," Santino says, "I say good night. I'm going out for the evening."

"Out?" I say. "Where?"

He raises his eyebrows. "Can't I have a private life?" he says. "Or are you the only one who's allowed to catch a lady's eye around here?"

"Oh, come on," I say. "Get out of here."

"Mark my words," he says. "Belle cares for you." I secretly hope it's true.

Santino leaves, and I dig right in to my dinner, but my mind is spinning. *Can Belle possibly care about me?*

I'm not charming, or funny, or even clean. Let's face it, I haven't showered, brushed my hair, or changed my clothes in . . . well, too long. I've been a monster to her.

BELLE

~18~

I don't know if I've ever felt this tired. When I get home from the hospital, planning to treat myself to a short, hot bath before turning in for the night, I put the book from Carlo on the table by the door.

Then I hear voices. I peek into the living room, and I'm surprised—and not happy—to find that Dad has company. It's company Dad hasn't had in a very long time.

"Hello, Belle," says his guest. I know him

at once. He's young and good-looking, but he's the kind of guy who knows how good-looking he is. Totally annoying.

"Hello, Francis," I say. I force a smile.

"Sit down, darling," Dad says, patting the couch beside him.

I reluctantly sit down. Francis was Dad's assistant until the business went belly-up. I haven't seen him or heard his name since, so something serious must be happening.

"What are you doing here, Francis?" I ask. I'm tired and in no mood for entertaining.

Francis laughs, like my rudeness is adorable. "How have you been, Belle?" he asks, crossing his legs. He picks up the glass from the table beside him—scotch from Dad's last bottle.

I shrug. "I'm tired," I say. "I should really get to bed. Tomorrow's another long day."

"About that," Francis says. He takes a sip. "I'm here to help."

"What?" I say, glancing at Dad.

"I called Francis last night," Dad admits. "I told him what happened. He's studying law now, so he can help."

I roll my eyes. "We don't need help," I say.

"On the contrary," Francis says in his most arrogant tone. "I've been in touch with your father's lawyer. She's already on her way to the Mostro household."

"What?" I say, leaning forward. "Why?"

"Did you think forcing a girl of fifteen to work tirelessly for the theft of a single rose was legal?" Francis says, smiling like a cat. "But not to worry. We'll put a stop to it." He stands and so does Dad. "The car's out front," Francis says.

"Where are you going?" I say, getting up and grabbing Dad's arm. "To Carlo's house?"

"Please," Dad says quietly, taking my shoulders in his hands. "Don't make this more difficult than it needs to be."

"It doesn't need to *be* at all," I say. "Just stay out of it!" I add, glaring at Francis over Dad's shoulder. He doesn't even look back at me.

"We should hurry," Francis says.

"Of course," says Dad. "You wait at home, Belle. You're exhausted anyway. Get some sleep."

The two of them shuffle out the door.

I rush to my bedroom and grab the phone. I dial the Mostros' number—it was printed on that tow truck receipt along with the address. But the operator comes on. Our phone's been disconnected except for emergencies. Dad hasn't paid the bill in months.

"Great," I say to myself, tossing the phone to the floor and heading back to the living room. Short of catching the train to the beach and then two buses that, for all I know, don't run this late, I'm stuck.

I see the book from Carlo still sitting on the table by the door, so I bring it into the living room and sit in Dad's chair. It smells like Dad—it always does—but now it also smells strongly of Francis and that awful cologne he wears.

I flip open the cover. For the first time, I notice the writing there, the scrawl of a teenage boy.

Belle,

Having you at the house the past few days has been great. You've been like a beautiful sunrise after a long, dark night. I'm sorry I've been such a beast.

I hope we can stay in touch once you're gone.

— Carlo

At the bottom, he left his email address.

* * *

I hurry across the street to the café, connect to their Wi-Fi, and type in Carlo's email address on my video chat. It rings and rings, but no one picks up.

CARLO

19

Santino's been gone for an hour or so, and the dinner he made was pretty delicious. Since then, I've watched about half of some animated movie I've seen before. I'm just about to doze off, thinking about Belle, when the doorbell rings.

"Mom!" I shout, as if she'd hear me in this huge house. She might not even be home. With a groan, I get up from the couch and hurry to the door. The doorbell rings again.

"I'm coming, relax!" I bark. I pull open the door. In shoves Mr. Beaumont. "What are you doing here?" I say, but before he answers, another man grabs me by the collar of my sweatshirt and slams me up to the door. My head bangs hard against it.

"Hey!" I shout. "Get off me!"

"You're in a lot of trouble," the man says. He has a wicked glare, and he's taller than me.

Just then, a woman wearing a suit and carrying a briefcase walks up behind him.

"Belle has been so depressed," Mr. Beaumont says. "Having to come here every morning. She says you're a monster. Shouting at her. Threatening her with violence."

"I never—" I start to say, but the other guy throttles me again, slamming my head against the door. "Ow!"

The woman with the briefcase pops it open and pulls out an envelope of legal papers. "This outlines the Beaumonts' case against the

Mostros," she says, holding it out. The tough guy grabs it and shoves it against my chest.

"The Department of Labor will be in touch," she adds. "Let him go, Francis."

Francis lets me go. Right onto the ground. The two men step over me, and the three of them leave. I don't even get up. Why bother?

I can't believe I imagined that Belle would like me. I'm mortified that I gave her that book. Has she read that sappy message I wrote in the front? I hope not. I can't believe I thought she and I were getting along.

And now she's sent these three after me, like a horde of villagers carrying torches and pitchforks to a monster's castle on the hill.

* * *

My spirit is bruised. My ego is bruised. I'm pretty sure my neck is bruised, too. But I'm not in the basement. I'm in my bedroom—my *real* bedroom.

Belle propped the family photo against a couple of action figures on my desk. She must have done it after crying over how pathetic my life is.

Staring at the picture, I realize it's not just my father I miss. It's also my mom. I miss the mom I had back then—before Dad got sick and before she started going to these all-night parties to try to forget her sadness. I miss myself, too. I miss enjoying life and enjoying books. I miss jumping in the ocean before breakfast and splashing around. I didn't do that once this summer.

I'm staring out the window now. The moon is high and full, reflecting in the wild ocean waves. My laptop starts beeping. An incoming video call. I don't recognize the username, but I answer it. And there she is—Belle. I quickly end the call and snap my laptop shut. It beeps again a moment later, but I don't care.

I hope I never see her again.

BELLE

~20~

I catch the last train to the beach. All I can do is hope that the buses are still running this late.

When I arrive at the station, I run to the bus schedule posted on the wall. It's faded and hard to read.

For a few seconds, I convince myself the last bus is at two a.m., but I know I'm kidding myself. It says midnight—there's no doubt. The last bus is already gone.

"Ciao, Bella!" shouts a familiar voice from a blue car, "What are you doing here?"

"Santino!" I shout, running to the curb. "Am I glad to see you. Can you give me a lift to the house?"

"I'm headed there!" he says. "Get in."

I climb in, and he pulls away from the curb. "What are you doing here?" he says.

"I have to see Carlo," I say. "Don't make me explain."

Santino coughs. "You don't have to explain," he admits. "He called me, interrupted my date night. He told me everything."

I stare at my hands. "Then you must think I'm horrible," I say.

"If you came out here to see Carlo," Santino says as we turn into the driveway of the mansion, "then you can't be as horrible as he believes."

Santino lets me in the front door before

parking the car. "He's in the basement," he says, pushing the door open.

"Thank you, Santino," I say before running into the house, through the kitchen, and knocking on the basement door.

"Carlo!" I shout. I try the door—it's locked. "Carlo, it's Belle. Please let me in!"

No reply. Maybe he's not even down there.

Santino comes in through the back door. "Won't he let you in?" he says.

I shake my head. "It's locked. Maybe he's asleep."

Santino pounds on the door with his fist. "Carlo," he says, like an angry father. "Open this door at once." He turns to me. "It doesn't have a lock. I don't know why it won't open."

Santino tries again. "I'll break this door, Carlo," he shouts. But still no response.

"Look out, Belle," Santino says. He steps back from the door and charges. The door flies

open, and a chair that had been jamming the door closed falls down the stairs.

I hurry down the steps and find Carlo sitting on the floor, hugging his knees, and shaking with sobs.

I drop down beside him while Santino waits at the top of the stairs. With my arm around his shoulder, I say, "Carlo, please don't cry. I never said any of the horrible things they told you. I didn't want them to come here tonight."

My cheeks are wet, and I realize I'm crying, too. "Please, Carlo," I say. "I like coming here. Even if I didn't have to clean, I'd come out here anyway. I'd come to see Santino, and—and to spend time with you."

I lay my head on his shoulder and listen to his sobs. "I'm sorry, Carlo," I say. "I'm sorry they treated you like this. I care about you," I say. "I understand you."

CARLO

21

"What?" I ask in shock. Belle shrugs. The tiniest smile appears on her lips.

"I guess I said I care about you," she says.

"But *why?*" I say. "I've been awful."

"Not too awful," she says. "I think you're very thoughtful when you want to be."

"I'm not beautiful," I say, "like you are."

She blushes a bit. "But you are," she says. "You have beautiful eyes, and I like your wild hair." She pushes it back from my eyes. "But more than that, you have beauty inside. I can see it, even if you can't right now." I guess Santino was right. Belle was going to break the curse.

* * *

When I wake up the next morning in my real bedroom, the first thing I see is the ocean. Then I see the photo. Instead of making me cry, it makes me smile.

I miss Dad. I always will. But I still have Mom, and I can help her remember that she still has me. I get up and find clean clothes. I shower and brush my hair back from my forehead.

Santino grins when I walk into the kitchen. "What?" I say with a smile. But I know what he's staring at: me, out of my basement and out of my misery.

Then Belle comes into the kitchen. Her hair is in a ponytail, and her face is flush with sleep.

"Good morning," I say. I almost run to her.

She takes my hand and says, "You look nice. You even smell nice." She gives me a quick hug.

"Come on, come on," Santino says, clapping twice. "We need to get moving."

We run out to the car, and a few minutes later, we pull up to the Beaumonts' house. Mr. Beaumont sees Belle first, and the relief on his face is obvious. An instant later, he sees me behind her, and his face turns red with rage.

"Dad," she says sternly, "you have to stop the legal action against Carlo's family."

"I can't do that," Mr. Beaumont says. "Once you get the ball rolling on things like this . . . the law is complicated, darling."

Belle takes a deep breath and says, clear as a bell and twice as loud, "I like him."

"What?" Mr. Beaumont says. He's looking right at her, stunned. I can't help smiling.

"I like him," she says, reaching for my hand.

"And what do you have to say?" he asks me.

"I like her, too," I say. She grins at me. "Isn't it obvious?" I say, smiling back at her.

He looks up at us and sighs. Belle looks at him and says, "Is it so terrible, Dad?"

Mr. Beaumont watches us holding hands in front of him, both of us looking happier than we have in a long, long time. "All right," he says. "I'll call off the attack lawyers right away."

Belle drops my hand and throws her arms around her father. "Thank you!" she says.

"I owe you an apology," I continue. Mr. Beaumont looks at me. "And quite a lot more than that," I go on. "I mistreated you. I was violent." *It's like I was a different person,* I think. *No, not even a person. An animal. A beast.*

"And for the last few days," I go on, "your daughter, who deserves so much better, cleaned my house." I look at Belle and add, "I shouted at her. I owe you both. And I intend to pay it back in full and with interest. A lot of interest."

"How will you do that?" he asks.

"I'll speak to my mom," I say. "Once I tell her that Belle—the girl I care about—is in need, I know she'll be happy to help."

Mr. Beaumont is hesitant. "Charity?" he says. "I don't know . . . I don't like the idea of accepting charity."

"Then think of it as payment to Belle for her hard work," I say. He's still unsure. "I also physically attacked you. So you could even think of it as an out-of-court settlement."

Mr. Beaumont laughs. "If that's the best you can do," he jokes, "then thank you. I'm sorry I misjudged you."

"You didn't," I admit. "I was a beast. But thanks to Belle, I'm not a beast anymore."

I put my arm around her. "You're beautiful," I say to her, looking into her storm-colored eyes.

She smiles and says, "So are you."

Beauty and the Beast

•★•★•

Beauty and the Beast is a French fairy tale. Jeanne-Marie Le Prince de Beaumont wrote the most well-known version of the story in 1756, *La Belle et la Bête*.

Beaumont's version introduces a wealthy merchant who has three daughters. Belle, his youngest, is the prettiest and most kind of the three. While the older two ask their father for expensive gifts, Belle simply asks for a rose.

After losing his ship in a storm, the merchant is suddenly very poor. Seeking shelter, he goes into the Beast's palace. It is there he finds the most beautiful rose he's ever seen, and he picks it for Belle, enraging the Beast. Only if he promises to return will the Beast allow him to take the rose. He promises to come back, and he brings the rose to Belle.

When Belle finds out where the rose came from, she goes to the castle herself. The Beast immediately falls for her and invites Belle to stay and be the mistress of the castle, and he, her servant. The two form a strong friendship, and soon the Beast asks Belle to marry him. She refuses, as she keeps dreaming about a handsome prince, but he continues to ask.

After months of this, Belle visits home. She uses a magical mirror to spy on the Beast and finds him lying on the ground, dying from heartbreak. Belle returns to the castle and tells the Beast she loves him. When her tears fall on him, he transforms into the handsome prince that Belle has been dreaming about.

Tell your own twicetold tale!

•★•★•

Choose one from each group, and write a story that combines all of the elements you've chosen.

A girl who wants to be a warrior

A king who has never met his son

A princess who runs away

An elf who wants to be king

A cloak

A fancy watch

A cupcake

A pineapple

A haunted house

A palace

A barn

An apartment

An annoying sister

A ghost

An angry queen

A smart baby

A tiger

A rabbit

A snake

A parrot

25th-Century US

A village in Russia

China

London, England

about the author

Olivia Snowe lives between the falls, the forest, and the creek in Minneapolis, Minnesota.

about the illustrator

Michelle Lamoreaux is an illustrator from southern Utah. She works with many publishers, agencies, and magazines throughout the US. She currently works out of Salt Lake City, Utah.